Innocent Times.

By

Gemma Owen-Kendall

To Jayne
Appreciate the support,
you are - unicontastic,
Happy Reading
Best Wishes
Gemma
x

Message from the author.

First, I would just like to say thank you for taking the time to read my debut book, I hope you enjoy my collection of YA Short Stories. I have been reading YA fiction since the age of fourteen and have always wanted to write my own stories under this category. I always loved writing stories when I was in primary school then continued with this into secondary school, one of my favourite subjects in school was English. My primary school teacher Mrs June Evans (who I have dedicated this book to) said to me, I had such a wild imagination, she always loved to read my stories. The royalties I receive from this anthology, I will make a donation in December to the Book Trust Charity.

In loving memory of my Nana, Patricia Jacqueline Turner, it is thanks to you why I love to read books.

In loving memory of my Primary School Teacher, Mrs June Evans, it is thanks to you why I have chosen to have a hobby in writing

Contents.

Girl with the Unicorn Hair

Grace.

The night started off so well; I was on a night out with my best friend Charlie, there was a warm feeling in the air as it had been a hot summers day, England was having a forever feeling heat wave that had no intention of ending soon. Not even my magical Parma violets gin and lemonade on the rocks was cooling me down. However, I admired the colour of my drink, it was like a lilac potion complimenting the run-down looking bar table. The drink also suited my unicorn hair colours of pink, blue, purple and silver, everyone always stopped me and asked how I get my unicorn hair so perfect. What nobody realises is that my hair is real, I live in a secret realm on Earth with my race who are known as The Unicorn People. The females are all born with the colours of the unicorn hair, but the males are all born with pure white hair. Our enemies were the Demon People but the Demon King and my father of the Unicorn People have a peaceful treaty that we live in harmony but our races are to never mate with each other. The kings allow our races to live in the realm of the mortals just as long as the enchanted realm is never revealed to the humans.

I gazed down at the table and saw how various markings appeared on the stained wood; I brushed my middle finger nail over one marking, curious to know whether if it was a scratch mark or chip or maybe both but I thought these tables at the bar could do with a makeover and some TLC. I reached for my drink again and the cool liquid soothed my dry throat but only for a moment as that dry tickly feeling soon came rushing back again. My eyes glanced over to the girl sat on the same table as me, her left arm has the beautiful colours of purple and turquoise; I watched the colours and noticed they are two wonderful tattoos of butterflies. Previously I have never noticed them properly until this very day, as I stared down at her tattoos I noticed the music in the background change to some keyboards, guitars and chimes which caused me to go into a daze of imaging I am a butterfly fluttering about in a haze to the rhythm of the music.

"Grace don't, not here as the humans will see." I came to my senses as the girl next to me was in fact my best friend and guardian, Charlie. I hadn't realised my powers had created the butterflies. It is often hard as the princess of the Unicorn People mixing into the mortal realm. Before I fully come to my senses Charlie slapped me. It worked as the butterflies soon vanished and luckily nobody had seen a thing. However, a throbbing to my left cheek shot straight through me. "Ouch you bitch." Was all I could say to her, but I also just nearly jeopardised the existence of the Unicorn People. "I think a thank you is in order. What would your father say if he knew what you just did?"

I was grateful my father had requested Charlie to be my protector. She was strong and fearless but also so kind and caring. Charlie had trained up to be a guardian for the royal family of the Unicorn People and was given the honour to be my personal protector. Her job was to accompany me every time I entered the mortal realm, this was often on nights out as I loved to go drinking in bars and enjoying a good dance in the clubs, I was eighteen years old so it was natural for me to be out enjoying myself a lot. Charlie loved our nights out, but she was often worried we were always being watched by someone so her guard was always up if anyone approached me or came near me. I can recall on one of the last times we were out two lads about my age approached me and to scare them off as she feared they would be no good for me, she kissed me passionately. Well, I appreciated all she did for me but sometimes I wished I could have gone off with a human boy for a moment or two. But because I am different to humans, things would never work out further than a kiss as I would jeopardise who I truly am.

Suddenly, this particular night out changed rapidly.He came and took me to his bedsit. The only guy I have ever loved and still do.He betrayed me and now I was under his charm spell. His name was Dominic, and he was the son of the Demon King. I fell in love with him when I was only sixteen and he was twenty-one.

I first met Dominic when I was swimming by a waterfall in the enchanted forest of our realm, I loved swimming as it always relaxed me and whisked me away from knowing I was a princess to just feeling like a normal person.

No one knew where I would disappear to, so I was always alone until that very day I met Dominic. I remember it so well as I had fallen completely in love with him but also it was like my heart was ripped out from my chest. I know it was crazy to fall in love with someone straight away but I had seen him often from a distance away when we had to visit each other's kingdoms to keep up with our peace treaty. My Father had forbidden me to speak with him and from the way Dominic always distant himself from me, I believed his Father had done the same about me. On this very day, I had just had a fallout with my father as he wanted to organise an arranged marriage for me to marry a nobleman of our people but I was not having any of this. I had lost my mother when I was a baby and I was not prepared at the tender age of sixteen to have my life planned by the king. The argument was that heated he threw his drinking glass of wine in my direction which only just missed me by an inch, things went too far that day and I ended up running out the kingdom to my secret location in the enchanted forest. It was such a beautiful and magical forest, it sparkled in the creases of the sunlight. If you looked close enough, you could see the forest fairies fluttering around. I always felt so safe and tranquil here. I ran as fast as I could to the waterfall, I wiped my teary-eyed cheeks and gazed down at the stream to my reflection, my Unicorn hair had changed to one colour, blue which was a sign of sadness. I gazed further down the stream in the waterfall's direction and wished for my father to change his mind. Rumour has it that the waterfall possessed magical wishing powers, so on this very day I had hoped my wish would come true.

I removed my gown and undergarments to take a swim to help relax my mind, I stepped into the cool flowing water that felt so soothing against my pale white skin. I had noticed by my reflection that my hair turned back to the original multiple colours that it should be. I took a few steps further into the water to my waist when I heard a branch snapping, worrying that someone had seen me as I was, I turned around towards the direction of the sound and quickly gathered my hair to cover my chest. "Who goes there?" I yelled, and hoping it was just my imagination from the start. From behind a nearby bush Dominic appeared wearing only a pair of shorts, I felt my insides burn up with embarrassment and yet I could not take my eyes off him. His skin was tanned so nicely as though he spent most days sunbathing, my eyes wondered along his ripped chest and torso. You could tell he was the son of the Demon King.

"Oh Dominic, my lord, please forgive me. I am not dressed appropriately for your presence." I had never said a word to him before and this was all I could scrabble out to him, I would have been surprised if he understood a word I had just said to him.

"Princess Grace, please, it should be myself apologising to you. I should not be spying on you."

Dominic spying on me? Really? How did he know where I was and I wondered if there had been many times he had watched me from this same spot every time I came here and seeing me swim? I turned my head away from him, feeling so ashamed of myself and for being so careless for not double checking I was alone. He walked right over to the edge of the stream, I felt his presence close by to me but I still could not look at him.

"Please princess, please do not look away from me, I am sorry I have startled you." His voice sounded so gentle and soothing.

"I am sorry my lord, I can't. I feel so embarrassed right now."

"I will close my eyes so you can dress again."

As promised he did so, I kept my gaze onto him whilst I reached for my over coat just to cover myself, he didn't peak at me or so I thought he didn't. The water dripped from my cool flesh.

"My lord, you can now open your eyes."

He slowly opened up his eyelids and revealed the colour of hazelnut brown eyes, I could feel myself being drawn into his gaze. He was even more handsome up close. I forgave him for spying on me, as we got chatting to each other I discovered he had also found this same spot and it was here that he also had to clear his mind, from knowing he was of royalty and wanted to feel like he was a normal person, the same reasons why I came here. That afternoon I had learnt so much about the Demon Prince, he was in the process on purchasing a place to stay in the mortal realm as he wanted to live there for a bit whilst his services weren't required in the kingdom of the Demon People. But he knew one day he would have to become king as he was the only heir to the throne. I had been to the mortal realm twice and had often wondered what it would be like to live there. He had a charming smile that was complimented with two dimples on his right cheek that caused me to go all weak at the knees and nearly making me drop my over coat.

"I have been watching you come here for quite some time princess, you are so very beautiful for a young lady." I blushed again and I was made to feel so special.

"Can I see you again, my lord?"

"Princess, meet me here tonight?"

I nodded as I was hoping I could meet him again like this in secret just the two of us, it was forbidden but at that moment in time I did not care what my father thought but I hoped he would not find out about this. Before Dominic left me he placed his soft lips onto mine, it was so nice and gentle, my first ever kiss with a boy and it was the Demon Prince. It might have sounded crazy,but I fell for him after our first proper meeting. When he left, I gathered my belongings, I even ensured I was dressed correctly and headed back to the kingdom of the Unicorn People. For the rest of the day I could not get Dominic out of my mind, this had been the first time a guy had been so close to me and had kissed me but also doubt sprung to mind, what if he had not enjoyed the kiss and would not turn up tonight? Worry stung me like a bee sting thinking if he would be waiting for me by that gorgeous waterfall.

I had not passed my father for the rest of that day, I just assumed he was living up to his royal duties as king by spending time outside our castle within the kingdom, thinking of him just bought back the hurt from earlier about how angry he was because I refused to have an arranged marriage. I was still so young, a virgin and there was so much more I wanted to do with my life, travelling the entire world visiting the unique countries on this planet and finding the other realms was something my heart desired. My father would still be king for many more years yet so a suitor for me could wait. But after seeing Dominic that day it drew me to him, there was just something about this dangerous boy that I was so attracted to.

Evening soon came around, I dressed myself appropriately like a princess should tonight in my gown made of the finest silks, tonight's colour was blue and purple. Pink was my favourite colour, but I wore it too often so as I did not know what to expect I just dressed up how I should on a royal social. I strolled cautiously to the enchanted forest in the hopes to have not been seen by anyone heading straight to the waterfall, the forest glowed at night so beautifully and peacefully, as I approached towards the waterfall, a forest fairy fluttered by gracing me with her charms. It was like she knew what I was doing and who I was meeting, but accepted it. I could not see Dominic to begin with and feeling disappointed with myself I perched onto a nearby rock and gazed over to the waterfall.

"Psst...... Princess, is that you?." He whispered at me close by.

"Yes, my lord, I am here waiting for you."

There he was right by me, clothed in his royal suit and boots, he looked perfect for such a dangerous boy, the prince of the Demon People. Again, I could not take my eyes off him and still, only drawn to him.

"Please, when it is just ourselves, let's be on a first name basis."

I blissfully smiled at him to show I agreed with him, he was so much taller than me and his frame was twice the size of mine, if our parents could have allowed us to be together I knew he would protect me.

"I see you're now fully dressed Grace on this occasion." The cheek of it.

"Well how many times have you been watching me when I come here?"

"I think I have lost count." He smiled at me, I was so curious about him and without focusing on my emotions my hair glowed a dazzling pink, I had never seen my hair do this before but from my understanding, it could only mean one thing. I had fallen in love with the Demon Prince.

"Wow, your hair its magnificent, what is happening?" he reached for a stem of my hair with two fingers and brushed them along it. How could I tell him what I was feeling, this was just so wrong and yet it felt so right being in his presence. There had only ever been one situation in history when a Unicorn boy had fallen for a Demon girl which had ended up in war over the two species and if we get caught now, it could bring another war. Dominic pulled me closer to his embrace, I liked the feel of his arms wrapped around me.

"Grace, I hope you don't mind me asking you this and forgive me if I over step the mark but I can't help but feel you are pure, have you not laid with anyone?"

Such an awkward question to ask, I had always thought about my first time and wondered what it would be like to choose a mate for my first time.

"I am pure."

"Wow just wow you are so exquisite Grace, I just can't resist myself for you. I want you, just all of you. I have seen how much you have blossomed over the years, seeing you grow to be the young lady you are today at the tender age of sixteen. I have been waiting for you to be the right age for this, in the hopes you will lay with me."

I just did not know what to say and answer back to him, I just wrapped my hands round the back of his neck and pulled my lips to his. I felt his hands rub down to the small of my back. Then the sound of footsteps approached at us in the distance, we were no longer alone. The prince's guardian, Michael, had found us together, he had been sent to look for Dominic under the command of the demon king.

"Dominic, your father requests your urgent attendance in the dining hall, he asks you to bring along the princess too."

"Oh shit... how did he find out." He barked at Michael.

"He spotted you on his hunt entering the forest. Then not far behind was the princess, stepping gently in the same direction.

Dominic clung to me tightly for a moment then he let go, Michael escorted us both to the kingdom of the Demon People towards the castle of the Demon King. Dominic walked a couple of steps behind me which made me feel slightly uncomfortable but it was the right thing to do as we could not show his people we had been together. Both him and Michael made it look like I was popping in for a visit to see the king himself. The kingdom of the Demon People applauded and bowed down as I walked on by, I nervously smiled, but more worryingly I could feel inside of myself ,wondering, if anyone else knew I had been with the prince. We approached the palace, the king's guards cleared a pathway to the doors. As always, the kingdom of the Demon People always felt so doom and gloom but always so warm as there were fires lit up on every single lantern and fire pit. The sun hardly ever shone over the kingdom, so the fires were a substitute to bring light.

The King wore his crown, it was made of black gold and jewels with a replica of a pair of demon horns on either side. Like his son, he was broad and muscular, the Demon Queen was beautiful with her jet black hair and well-toned physique. No wonder the Demon Prince was so good looking, having inherited both his father's build and his mother's looks. However, they were not happy to see me.

"Princess Grace, thank you for taking up my invitation for a visit but I am afraid it is not on acceptable terms." The king came across stern but kept a straight face, I went down to my knees and dropped my head in shame.

"Father it is not her fault." I heard Dominic defend me to his father, "I asked her to meet up with me." The prince was defending me, but I could tell he did not want to disappoint his father anymore.

"You both know this could jeopardise the peace between both Kingdoms, I am ashamed of you my son and Grace you should know better than to betray your Father." He said sternly to us both, he was so right on everything but I could tell he would give us both a chance, I hope he would agree to us meeting up in secret still without my father knowing. I just could not go through with an arranged marriage as it is, especially to someone I do not know.

"My lord, my lady, I ask of your forgiveness." My hair was still the colour of pink, the Queen noticed and instantly knew straight away. She got up off her chair and approached me. She held out her hands for me to take them and help me to stand up. She stroked my hair, took a whiff of my essence, and smiled at me.

"You are in love with my son."

I turned to look at Dominic who then looked away from me but towards the direction of his father.

"Is this true?" the king questioned me, he stood up from his throne and joined his wife gazing down at me.

"Yes." I whispered with teary eyes "It is true." I could not hold back the tears anymore, I dreaded Dominic finding out about this, I did not want him to know I had fallen in love with him.

"I love her." I was not expecting Dominic to say this. "I have loved her since the day she was born, I love her to watch over her and see her grow to blossom into a beautiful young lady that she is right now."

The king walked over to his son and placed his hand onto Dominic's right shoulder.

"I am sorry I can't allow you to be together, this kills me to say this but Dominic you have to make a choice. You can either choose to be with Grace and be banished from the kingdom or you must end this affair with Grace and choose to never meet her again unattended."

I did not like the sound of this, but I sort of hoped Dominic would follow his heart and live a life with me. We could have run away together to live in the mortal realm, away from everything, and start our own lives living as normal people. I could have seen it happening right now until what I heard next broke my heart.

"Grace I love you but I am so sorry, I have chosen to stay with my father and my people. Please forgive me."

I crumpled to the floor crying my heart out, my hair turned all black. That had only happened once before when I was very young and losing my mother. I heard footsteps trying to approach me coming from Dominic's direction, but then he was held back by his guardian, Michael. The Demon Queen went over to me and kneeled by the beside me. She brushed away some of my tears and held me for a moment.

"I am so sorry Grace, remember I love you but we can't be together." Were the last words I heard Dominic say to me, Michael released him and the Demon Prince left. It was the last time I saw him until now, two years later….

My bodily urges took control upon me, telling me to go with him and be under his command. Charlie, bless her, tried to protect me, she tried her hardest to keep me safe and sacrificed her soul to not let any harm come to me but he was too smart and cunning. His friend and guardian Michael removed the soul from her body, I remembered vaguely her silhouette drifting to me on her last ounce of power and strength but she had to let go.

Charlie was no longer my protector, my best friend gone, forever.

Now I was here with him and we were alone, he kidnapped me and took me away to his bedsit. Dominic unbuttoned his shirt revealing a toned torso. He knelt over me on his bed and kissed me passionately. All the anger for Charlie vanished as soon as his lips touched mine and all the hate I had for him released away from me. All I wanted now was to enjoy this moment with him, sparkled and changed to pink, my powers for love for him revealed once again.

He stopped kissing me, gazed into my eyes and stroked my brightly lit up hair. I knew what he wanted from me but I wasn't sure if I was ready to go on to this, my first time. What would everyone think of me? The chosen unicorn girl with the demon boy. Good and evil together.

Charlie.

I t honoured me the day when the king of the Unicorn People requested that

I, Charlie, would be the protector of his daughter Grace. We were of similar age so as children we had often played together in the palace court yard, the kingdom of the Unicorn People was always so bright and a haven to be. Our allies were the evil ones known as the Demon People but we had a friendly truce with them and once you got to know their king and queen, they were friendly. Their son Dominic however, I was just unsure about him, there was just something about him I felt was not right. I noticed how he always looked at Grace like he was a predator stalking his prey until that very moment he would attack. I knew he wanted her but he could not have her, it was forbidden.

The two kings always got on so well every time they visited each other and they both could put on a right party and feast. His highness,the Unicorn King wore a wondrous crown, it was golden and glittery and in the middle where it all joined was the Unicorn horn. The horn was a symbol of our sacred being, the animal of the Unicorn herself, who could transform herself to become one but also be a person to. However, there has been no-one else able to do this unless you were the chosen one. I believed it worried the king that his daughter could do this someday, that she was the chosen one.

I remember when Grace was sixteen she had come home one night very upset, I knew there had been problems with her father as he wanted her to have an arranged marriage to a nobleman but she was not having any of it. Her parents fell in love off their own back and that is what Grace wanted to do, but unknown to his daughter, the king was worried that she would have the same fate as her mother. So, he wanted to ensure, Grace was looked after and cared for by someone of noble birth. Not by someone who was too focused on ruling a kingdom like himself as he could not fulfil being a husband. No one knew who or why the queen passed away but the king felt so guilty about this.

Grace had told me about her encounter with the Demon Prince and how she had fallen madly in love with him, even two years later I knew she still cried for him and struggled to get over him. When Grace was eighteen, the king finally gave me the role as her protector, I had been training up for this moment since I was a child. We were already friends but yet, inside I loved her and wanted to be the one to protect her, we were like sisters as she was an only child. This very night I couldn't save Grace, I tried so hard but Dominic was one step ahead of me, I knew he had still been stalking Grace. This very night I had taken her out to the mortal realm to dance the night away and to forget all about the Demon boy. He crushed her heart by choosing to serve the Demon King over his love for her. I was appointed by the king of the Unicorn People to protect his daughter at all costs, even if that cost me my life. Now here I was, stuck in the spirit world until they have granted me the chance to live again. Dominic's protector Michael, another Demon like the prince was too strong and powerful for me, he completely ripped my soul from my body and all I could do was sacrifice myself as he would have killed Grace. Luckily my soul struck down Michael before I drifted away into the spirit world. Please forgive me my king and my princess, we will meet again.

Dominic.

I have been watching her for so long, the only girl who I have ever loved, but I betrayed her. I chose to serve him, the demon king, my people were once at war with the unicorn folk until my father and their king put a truce together. Our fathers wanted to keep the balance between good and evil together in a peaceful harmony. How could I, the son of the demon king, fall for the princess of the unicorn people? I know I had broken her heart, but I could not help but follow her as often as I could. Although my male ego got the better of me, my head and my heart could not stop loving Grace.

She was on a night out with her best friend Charlie and to not make it look obvious I was following her, I asked Michael to accompany me to the club. Charlie spotted us straight away and instantly I realised that tonight was a terrible idea, we should not have come here and pretty much we should have stayed outside and watched the girls from a distance. Angrily Charlie slapped me across the face, Grace tried to reason with her, it was obvious she still loved me just as much as I still loved her. Michael triggered automatically to my defence but before I could stop him he tore away Charlie's soul out of her body. However the spark from such a murderous act destroyed Michael, Charlie sacrificed herself for the princess, her best friend. This was the same bond that I had with Michael.

I looked over at the princess. She was shocked and numb by what she had just witnessed, her best friend killed right in front of her. All I wanted to do was hold Grace and make all of this go away, but I wanted something else from her too which urged me to carry out my next plan, I wanted to take her innocence from her. I took Grace by the hand, she was reluctant to start off with but as to not cause a scene in the club she surrendered herself to me. My plan was already starting to work.

My bedsit was not too far away from the club, Grace slowly walked behind my pace but I would not release my grasp, I could sense she was crying but I was too ashamed to stop and look at her. I could not bear myself to look her in the eyes whilst she was crying. We entered my bedsit and straight away I dragged her to my bed.

The Imposter

The sunlight shone through my butterfly patterned curtains as I slowly woke up from a wonderful dream; I rubbed the sleep away from eyes and slowly sat up. There he was, sat at the edge of my bed, someone I did not know personally but knew of very well. I did not understand how he got into my dorm, never mind my bedroom and watching me sleep whilst sitting on the edge of my bed. I heard him breathing slowly, like his focus was just fixated on me and the smell of his aftershave lingering through the air.

He moved more onto my bed, trying to get closer towards me, but I hunched myself into a ball and held on tightly to my duvet. I could see on the expression of his face what he wanted to do to me, he smiled whilst gritting his teeth, his brown hair was gelled back smoothly, whereas normally when I have passed him on the street his hair appeared to be untidy. Now I had a closer look at my imposter, he was about the same age as me, nineteen maybe a year or two older and his eyes had a look of evil in them.

I never understood why he stalked me, for the past year he would appear at most student parties where I was at and always stood a distance away from me, watching me as though I was prey for his predatory fulfilments. When I had spotted him at these parties or in the street, he would always come across as being a loner but as I tried to never pay much attention to him, I could not have cared more or less if he had any friends or not, I just wanted him to stop stalking me. I had reported him often to the university faculty and on site security but there was nothing they could do as he had not harmed me in any way and had broken no laws, until now that is, waking up to find him sat on the edge of my bed.

"How did you get in?" I asked him.

"That is for me to know and for you to find out. Now I have you all to myself away from your friends, I have made sure no one can get in to help you now."

Fear struck me hearing him say those words to me, a chill of ice froze down my spine and yet the feeling of expecting this to happen one day

31

prepared myself for what my next course of action would be. I slowly reached for my knife under my mattress, trying not to make it too obvious to show him what I was about to do and in a rage of adrenaline pumping through me, I flew myself onto him…

Him

This short story is also in Monday At Six, first published in 2017. I also adapted this piece into a stage play that was performed at Louth Playgoers Riverhead Theatre in June 2018 by Hambledon Productions.

When I was a little girl, I always dreamt of love and having my own fairy tale story, my mother would often tell me back then that there is someone out there for everyone but she didn't mean from out there. My name is Kimberly and here is my story for what changed my life. You think boys during school are so complicated, well how about falling in with a boy who is not even from this world. The first day I started secondary school was when I first saw him, the guy I fell in love with that felt like it would be for all eternity, his name was Danny. He was always a few inches taller than the rest of the guys in our year, his chocolate brown hair was always spiked perfectly and often I was tempted to touch it to see how much gel he used to keep his hair in place. From time to time I often caught his eyes, those deep hazel brown eyes that developed butterflies in my stomach, causing me to stare at him for ages in class and because of this my grades at school weren't always the best. He never seemed to be interested in dating any of the girls in school, just about nearly every girl in school had asked him out for a drink, cinema or study date but he always declined. I never had the courage to even speak to him, never mind asking him out for a date. Although I had long blonde hair and blue eyes, I did not think of myself as very attractive, I never seemed to have any guys asking me out. This did not help my confidence, I guess you could even say I was not very popular with the boys at school, hardly any of them asked me out and as for parties and hang outs, I was rarely asked. I was happy though, and all I needed was my best friend Jessica to talk about situations with; she was pretty much my sister but from another family. Without Jessica, I would have been eternally on my lonesome.

When I started year ten, this was when I cracked on with my studies and forget all about

Danny and boys in general. Of course, I would never be rid of him as he was in a lot of the same classes as me but I was just sick of my parents constantly nagging at me about low grades and the teachers continuously telling me to do better. The nail on the head was when my parents got called into a meeting with my head teacher about how low my grades were and that I would soon go on to take my GCSEs, if I did not improve I would have to re-take another year. This meeting took place right at the end-of-year nine just before the summer break so I made a choice to myself and with the guidance from Jessica that during the six week summer break I would study ahead and try to improve my grades. In September going into year ten I was determined to do well and forget all about Danny. But who would know during this year at school that it would change my life for all eternity and this event happened at the yearly Christmas school masquerade ball.

My grades had progressed so as a treat to say, 'Well done' my parents let me attend the ball. The head teacher had personally hand delivered my invite to my parents, so they knew I was not making up a story that my grades had improved so well. I had gone shopping with Jessica to choose our dresses, it was a cool but dry day on that Saturday we picked our dresses, as an idea we visited the local bridal shop to see on the off chance there may be some bridesmaid gowns or prom dresses reduced. As luck would have it, I came across a silver ball gown. It was on display in the shop window. Silver was not a colour I would have normally gone for, but in the sunlight's reflection it shone and reflected beautifully through the window. It was like the dress was out of this world and I don't know what it was, but it drew me to it. Something made me want to enter the shop and check the price of it. It was as though I looked at it outside the shop in one moment and then the next, I was there standing right by it. There was just something about this dress that I could not get my head round but I loved it and I had to buy it. In my daze of excitement and confusion I reached for the yellow tag, it displayed reduced to £89.00. Mum had given me £100.00 to spend in town as a treat. I had seen a few CDs I wanted to treat myself to , but I loved the dress so much I sacrificed my treats and purchased the dress.

The lady in the dress shop was welcoming, she was an elderly lady but knew right away what I wanted but her welcome came across as though she knew who I was. She already had a few of the other girls from my school placing orders for dresses because of the ball, but not one of them wanted the silver gown. As it was on display in the window, the other girls had most likely thought it would cost a lot of money and not taken a second look at it. The dress was like it was meant to be for me. The lady smiled at me as she took my measurements and as a kind gesture, she let me have the silver eye mask with a butterfly on either side on it, free of charge that matched my new silvery dress. I was still not with it exiting the shop from my excitement about the dress, I walked straight into Danny who had been walking by, I lost my balance and began to fall to the ground. I closed my eyes as I prepared to hit the concrete paving from underneath, but I stopped in mid fall. A powerful arm had caught hold of me and then a hand stroked my cheek. The same feeling of the butterflies in my stomach happened again. I opened my eyes and was met with his gaze. We held each other for a moment just looking at each other, although there were no words to say it was amazing feeling his embrace.

"Erm sorry about that." I said to him, feeling like a complete idiot. "Must have been in a world of my own."

I let go of him and stepped away, I had completely forgotten about my friend Jessica and sure enough I had walked out of the shop before she even chose her own dress. I turned to look for her and smiled nervously as she stood in the doorway of the dress shop. She smiled joyfully back at me and then walked over to me. I am sure she must have seen what happened between Danny and I. He just looked at me again for a moment, nodded then walked away, not quite sure what that was all about but I still really liked him a lot, I had avoided thinking about him during the last few months and everything had come flooding back to me. I watched him walk away, noticing he did have a slight look over his left shoulder at me and then the next moment he was gone and no longer in my eyesight.

"What just happened there?" my friend Jessica curiously asked me

"I do not understand, but whatever it was I loved every moment of it."

She playfully nudged me and I playfully pushed her back then we carried on strolling through town linking arms, giggling away and just talking about him. It felt good to talk to her again about Danny and how much I still truly liked him, those feelings from when I first saw him the day we were all starting secondary school in year seven. Nobody knew nothing about his past as he had not gone to primary school with any of the pupils at secondary school. I can remember during the school holidays that year when a U.F.O had been spotted flying over our insignificant town, it was some kind of flying saucer like object hovering above like it was observing the area. I saw this flying object myself, as I did a late evening walk to and from the local shop and I could have sworn it hovered over me at one point, it was like whoever was inside it wanted to take a closer look at me. I remember there being a green illuminated light glowing underneath the object, the saucer itself was like a dark gun metal grey colour with red flashing lights round it. There was a loud humming sound as it hovered over me and since then I have longed to know who was inside of it. As I witnessed this alone, I had not shared my story with anyone apart from Jessica, I was thankful she believed me when I explain what I saw that night and how it looked. Since then Danny appeared on the scene starting secondary school the same time as myself, no one knew where he lived and he was always dropped off and picked up from school in a black Mercedes-Benz SUV with tinted out windows. I knew this as I walked past this vehicle one afternoon from school and just had to observe the vehicle in all its details. This mysterious side to him is part of the reason why I was so attracted to him. Deep down I thought he might have been one of the beings in the flying saucer that evening but I hoped he wasn't. The more I thought and spoke to Jessica about this, the more I thought how would an inter-galactic relationship ever work and then again, my idea of all this must have been my teenage hormones going into overdrive. Everything I spoke of this to was Jessica, she listened and often told me to turn this fairy-tale imagination of mine into a story about Danny being an alien and me falling in love with him.

The week of the school dance was when I found out Danny was not from round here, in fact he was not of this world. The incident happened at the masquerade ball. The school hall had been decorated with silver and white decorations from glittery snowflakes to fake snow sprayed across the tables. At the far side of the hall was the DJ booth and scattered round the ceiling we huge flashing disco lights, the centre of the ceiling had a gigantic disco ball that added a sparkle effect round the room. I was one of the last to arrive at the ball, I came with Jessica but all I was bothered about is if Danny would be there.

He was sat at a table on his own in a corner away from everyone else but it was like he wanted to watch out for someone, I walked over to join him, leaving Jessica chatting to a couple of guys in our school year. She winked, stuck her tongue out, but gave me the thumbs up when she noticed I wanted to go over to him. I was feeling nervous but swallowing the lump in my throat I headed over in his direction, passing bythe unmanned drinks table, I picked up a cup fall of punch. Not thinking why the drinks table was unsupervised, I sipped a mouthful of punch. As I began to walk over to Danny, I felt a burning sensation in my throat all the way down to my stomach, my throat then closed up preventing me to breathe. I was suffocating, my eyes felt heavy and my head was spinning, thoughts of my life ending was all I could think about. Someone had poisoned me.

Feeling like there was no hope, Danny appeared by my side looking worried. He held my hand and supported my balance. He laid me down underneath the nearest table, feeling his hand stroke my cheek as he whispered something into my ear.

"Stay calm, but I am going to make this go away."
I tried to look up at him to understand what he was saying, I was thinking how he could save me. I coughed up some blood, whatever he was going to do I hoped he would make it happen sooner as I did not want to die. Danny moved his face closer to mine and still stroking my cheek, I properly gazed into his eyes. They had lit up like they were glowing but they looked beautiful. He kissed me slowly and so gently, his lips felt so soft and smooth, I tried to kiss him back but I was too weak. I closed my eyes and everything went black.

The next morning, I woke up in my bedroom, my dress was hung up on my wardrobe. I couldn't remember how I even got home. But I remembered someone had tried to kill me and I was going to find out who it was.

The Text Message

This story was first published in Fish and Freaks, October 2018.

Jane had just woken up from an awful dream that felt like an actual life nightmare, this was the same re-occurring dream all week, the sweat dripped rapidly from her forehead taking in deep breaths to try calm down from her never ending nightmares. The dream was about a teenage boy her age; he had chocolate coloured brown hair and ocean blue eyes. The teenage boy looked very similar to her best friend Pete. She had witnessed that both of them were on the run from a couple of robbers trying to break into a nearby car. One of the robbers pulled out a gun from his faded denim jacket pocket and shoots at the callow lad. He falls to the ground clinging hold to his blooded chest fighting for his life, his last words to Jane are "Jane.... Run... don't worry about.... Me." At that very same moment Jane then opens her hazel eyes to the clock face showing 6:00am, wiping the sticky sweat from her forehead and stroking back her long blonde hair and thinking happy thoughts, she shuts her eyes again and drifts off into another heavy sleep.

Pete and Jane have been best friends since they were both very young, they both attended the same schools, secretly Jane had always hoped their friendship would blossom into something more romantic.   "Jane….
Jane….wake up, it's 10 'O'clock, Pete will be here in an hour." Her mother yells up the stairs to wake her up. Jane opens her eyes to see the time is actually 10am, and that she had managed to sleep for another four hours without having another nightmare. Like every Saturday morning Jane is in no hurry to get out of bed and chooses to lay in bed a little while longer, reaching for the bed-side table for the television remote she decides to finish watching the rest of her favourite film from the night before. Not long after the television is on her mother walks in with a cup of tea like she does for Jane most Saturday morning's, there were no other children to treat as Jane was an only child.

"Thanks   mum"   Jane   says   with   an enormous smile on her

"Don't expect it from me every Saturday morning" tells her mother with a big joking smile on her face. Her mother was unaware of Jane's re-occurring nightmares, although they had a close relationship, Jane chose not to worry her mother and keep it quiet. She couldn't t tell anyone, especially Pete. Jane gave her mother a hug before leaving Jane to watch her film. As her mother leaves Jane reaches for the bed-side table again but this time for her mobile phone. Jane switches on her phone, straight away a text message from Pete is received and as always the feeling of butterflies in her tummy appears again, the same feeling she always gets when Pete is around or texts her. Smiling away to herself she reads the message from Pete asking if their plans today will be perhaps a walk round town, Jane replies straight away accepting his idea. Realising the time, Jane finally decides to get up and sort herself out.

An hour later as Jane is getting ready, the doorbell rings, Jane hears her mum hurry to the front door and then inviting the person inside. "Jane… Jane… Guess who is here." Her mum always knows how to embarrass her.

Jane comes flying down the stairs to Pete and throws her arms round him for a hug. Pete hugs her back. "What's all this about?" he asks with a smile on his face.

"I am just looking forward to our plans today." Jane replies, giggling away. She then puts on her sketcher trainers, kisses her mum goodbye and they both walk out the house linking arms. They head towards the nearest bus stop to catch the next number three bus route into town. It was a dull overcast day and the air felt chilly for an April spring morning, Jane had hoped the sun would be out today to compliment what she hoped would be a romantic walk through town with the hopes of birds, butterflies and bees flying through the air. They both had not walked far from Jane's house when they spot a pair of crooks trying to break into a nearby car.

"HEY." Yells Pete at them without thinking and realising what he has just done "What do you think you are doing?" The two crooks stop what they are doing, the pair of them are wearing faded black hooded jackets and sunglasses to try to hide their identities, but they both look in the direction of Pete and Jane.

"Pete, I think this is a bad…."

"Ssshhhhhh Jane, I don't want this to go out of control." Interrupting her.

Then suddenly, the two men walk towards Pete and Jane. One of them is holding what appears to be a metal rod. The young teenagers hold each other's hands and start to run away in the opposite direction, the two robbers follow close behind them. Suddenly a gunshot is heard, Jane stops and hopes this is not her nightmare coming true. She looks at Pete, one hand is still holding hers and his other one is clasping his chest tightly as he collapses to the ground. The crooks stop running and watch Jane as she kneels down beside Pete, tears fall down her red cheeks. In Pete's last breath, he looks up at Jane and tells her to run.

Jane stands up and looks towards the two men. Her nightmare had come true but this was the part where it ended, she was not ready for what will happen next.

"You fucking bastards!" she screams at them.

Sirens are then heard in the distance. Instead of trying to help her and clear up what a mess they have done, the two men flee the scene. Jane sits down beside Pete again holding his hand, blood is pouring out of his chest rapidly. 'Who else saw this' she thought to herself, feeling numb and puzzled. The paramedics arrive and work quickly as they can to try save Pete's life, Jane Kisses Pete's fore head "You are safe now." She whispers in his ear and then let's go of his hand.

Jane stands up as they carry Pete on a stretcher into the ambulance. Tears fill her eyes, knowing full well that her reoccurring dream has now become a reality. 'Where the hell were the police? Why did they not show? This was the thoughts that came to mind as she climbed into the back of the ambulance. The quick trip to the hospital seemed like an eternity, continuously Pete was trying to fight for his life, in and out of cardiac arrest until there was no fight left in him.

At the hospital, Pete was whizzed through into an emergency room to be operated on. At the hospital Pete was whizzed through into an emergency room to be operated, Jane paced up and down continuously in the waiting room. The receptionist had called for Pete's mother to get to the hospital as soon as possible and to be by

Jane's side. Jane explained what had happened to her son but struggled with retracting that morning's event, she felt like it was her fault for arranging plans for them today. As Pete, would still be fine and not fighting for his life.

"Oh Jane, I am so sorry you had to witness that. I know you don't want to leave Pete but please go home and try to calm down. I will have someone to call your mum to come pick you up." Pete's mum said smoothly as possible trying to fight back the tears hearing the news of her son. Jane refuses her kind offer and chooses to walk home to try clear her head, the walk home took forever and Jane did not acknowledge anyone at all walking by, now and again she felt an icy sensation stroking down her spine but no one was close enough to her, maybe it was her imagination getting the better of her. She hoped her mother would be at home by the time she got back for someone to give her comfort and support but sadly no one was at home. In Jane's last ounce of strength, she slumped onto her bed and cried herself to sleep.

Jane was woken up by her mobile phone ringing.

"Hello, Pete is that you?" she asked before actually checking to see whose number it was calling her.

"No it's Pete's mum."

"How is Pete? Is he going to live?"

"That is what I have phoned to tell you about, he's…. dead." Pete's mum said, beginning to cry.

"What…. No… Why Pete?"

"He managed to tell me a message to pass on to you, he thinks you are a wonderful girl and friend but you must live on with your life."

"Thank you for letting me know. Bye."

"Bye."

The tears start to fall again down Jane's red hot puffy cheeks. All she could think about was the happy memories of her and Pete. The times when they went out to dinner together, the times they both had ice creams and fun in the sun, they were like a couple but not even romantically linked with each other. She wished she could tell Pete how she actually felt towards him and wanted to have her first proper kiss with him. Then suddenly her thoughts were interrupted by a text message on her mobile phone. The receiver is from

Pete's number. She reads the message, wondering who has got Pete's phone.

Don't forget me, I now know how your feelings are towards me, mine are also the same about you.

For a moment Jane freezes, trying to make heads and tails to what she has just seen. She reads the text message again and then again. Feeling confused and freaked out, she calls Pete's mum to see who is using his phone.

"Hello." Pete's mum answers sniffling from tears

"Hi, is that Pete's Mum?"

"Yes, is this Jane?"

"yes it's me."

"Oh.. hi Jane, what can I help you with?"

"I am sorry to ask this but I was wondering who has got Pete's phone?"

"No one has dear, I have put it in his room with all of his belongings."

"Oh, you see the thing is, this may sound crazy but I have just received a text message from Pete's phone."

"Oh… really, does it have time and date when it was sent?"

"It should have, I haven't yet checked that."

"Well keep it on your phone and I will pop round later this week to have a look at it."

"Yes that would be nice, see you soon. Bye."

After the phone call with Pete's mum, Jane lays back down on her bed again, this time thinking about the mysterious text message, wondering that she may be going crazy or could it be someone playing a joke on her? Her mobile phone bleeps again, receiving another text message from Pete's number.

This isn't a joke, it's really me, Pete. I have liked you since I first saw you all those years ago.

Jane wanted to see for herself if this was actually happening so decides to reply back to the message.

Is it really you? How can it be when you have died? How can you still text me?
She receives a reply straight away.

I can't explain at the moment, I will text you another time.

Jane then begins to cry again. This time she wasn't sure if these were tears of happiness or tears of sadness, she couldn't make her mind up as she was feeling all over the place. Her mum came home at the right time, Jane wanted a hug off her in the hopes it may take some of the pain away for a moment.

"Jane I heard what happened, I am so sorry love." Her mum holds her. "If you ever want anything, just ask and I will see what I can do."

"Thanks mum but all I want at the moment is Pete but I can't have that." Jane cries and holds her chest.

"I wish I could take this pain away from you Jane, I really do. Would you like me to do something nice for your tea?"

"No mum I am ok at the moment, I don't feel like eating."

Jane's mum felt helpless but to try to help her daughter she hugged her even tighter and stroked her hair. Jane cried into her mother's loving embrace until she drifted off to sleep.

A week had passed by since Pete's death. To Jane it had gone by in such a numbness blur. The day she dreaded had arrived, Pete's funeral, and this would be the day she would tell her final goodbye forever to the person who meant so much to her. Jane had not received any more text messages from

Pete's number but to try not let his memory fade away she had kept the ones she had received on the day he died. Pete's mum had not been round to see her either.

"Jane, sorry I haven't been round to see you, I am finding it really hard." Said Pete's mum

"That's ok, I understand."

"Have you still got that message you received from Pete's phone?"

"Yeah, I had received a couple more on the same day but nothing else recently."

"Well I will come over this week, I promise." Said Pete's mum with a brave smile on her face.

His mum walks off to attend the wake at the local pub down the road from the church, Jane isn't feeling up to seeing anyone so she walks to a nearby park and luckily for her there is no one around. She sits on the old rusted swing. The play area seemed to have stayed the same, since the park area was developed when she was an adolescent girl. Jane then has a vision of her and Pete talking while sitting on the same swings. This was something they both used to do a lot. A light breeze blew Jane's long blonde hair then suddenly her vision is interrupted by the feel of a frozen breath on the back of her neck. She turns around but no-one is there. Thinking she is going crazy she closes her eyes and takes a deep breath, Jane feels an icy cold kiss on her right cheek but still no-one else is around. Not knowing what is happening Jane leaves the park and walks home. It wasn't too far away only about half a mile.

As Jane walks into her house, she can faintly hear someone call her name that sounded like Pete's voice. Shaking her head to get a grip, she slams the front door shut and runs straight up to her bedroom. As respect to Pete and his family Jane had left her phone at home, however she was curious to see if any messages had been sent from Pete's number. Jane picks up her phone to have received a message as she had guessed.

Thank you for coming to my funeral, I am happy you decided to go. xx
Now Jane knew all this was actually happening, she was not losing her mind, and she didn't feel freaked out anymore. In fact, it made her happy and some of the pain go away. Not wanting this to end, she replied.

Was it you in the park with me today? The kiss? Xx.

Bleep bleep. **Yes, it was me xx.** Came the reply.

I wish I could have done it back but I couldn't see you lol xx.

Lol, well anyway you will be expecting something to happen tomorrow night when you are happily dreaming away. I can't tell you as it is a surprise xx.

The next day was Jane's 16th birthday, her original plans were to be going out with Pete to the cinema and Pizza afterwards but today Jane was not up to doing anything and just stay at home. All day long she was thinking what her surprise could be. Could it be Pete alive again? Would she wake up to a lot of money? She didn't have the slightest idea at all.

Jane snuggled down into her bed just after midnight, this evening she had been watching a couple of her new blu rays she had received today, it also helped her stop thinking about Pete and the surprise. As Jane closed her eyes and drifted off to sleep, she was somewhere nice and romantic, an enchanted forest that had a sparkling water. There was a bright moon in the night sky and a cool calming breeze in the air, Jane felt happy and safe in the forest. Then someone put their arms around her, it was Pete, Jane turned round and hugged him back, she was so happy to see him again.

"Where am I?" she asks

"Your dream place."

"Is this real?"

"To me yes."

"How did you get into my dream?"

"I am part of you now."

"But...."

"Sssshhhhhh now."

Pete then moves in to kiss Jane, she finally got her first ever kiss and the person who she wanted to share this first special moment with. It was what both of them wanted to do for so long and it finally happened. The moment ended as Jane woke up. This was the best birthday present she had received, kissing the boy of her dreams. Jane began to cry, but this time these were tears of happiness as she got to see Pete again.

The next morning Jane took a walk to the beach to where her and Pete used to sit on the cliff edge gazing down at the sea and watching the waves crash along the rocks. She stood on the cliff edge alone this time, just gazing away in the distance and thinking happy thoughts about her and Pete. Then her mobile phone bleeped again, it was another text message from Pete's number, she decides she will read it later on and hoped he was nearby watching over her.

Alternate Ending (From Fish and Freaks):

The next morning Jane decided to take a walk to the beach to where her and Pete use to sit on the cliff edge gazing down at the sea and watching the waves crash along the rocks. She stood on the cliff edge alone this time just gazing away in the distance and thinking happy thoughts about her and Pete. Then her mobile phone bleeped again, it was another text message from Pete's number, she decided to read it later on and hoped he was nearby watching over her. Then he was there standing right in front of her holding his hand out.

"Jane, you can have your wish and join me?" he whispered gently to her

"Will it hurt?" she asked him out loud, luckily no one was around to hear her what could have looked like she was talking to herself.

"Don't worry I am here with you every step you take." He sounded just like and angel.

"Oh I don't know, I can't leave my mother." Jane hesitated, she was not a person who could leave the close bond she had with her mother.

"but this is what you wanted, for us to be together again." The tone in Pete's voice had now changed and sounded forceful.

His hand reached her arm as Pete started to slowly drag Jane closer and closer to the edge. She was just one further footstep away to join an eternal life with Pete....

Witch

Since the day I '.. always been different to any human being; in fact, I am not a normal person. I was born a witch, but not the kind you see with black scraggly hair, a pointed hat, wart at the end of your nose and a broomstick. I look like any normal human with sapphire blue eyes, lips red like a rose, skin as pale as snow and long golden hair but I have a mark down my right arm, it looks like a birthmark as it is dark purple and disguises well as one until I use my powers when it glows like a light bulb. The mark is connected to my right elbow joint and goes down my arm and splits at my wrist connecting to my middle finger and my thumb. My parents have often told me the tale of my birth. My right arm was glowing brightly like a star and so my parents instantly knew I was different. My mother had seen the mark before on my great-grandmother, she had been a witch so my parents knew I was the next chosen one, that it was my destiny to help protect mankind from our enemies that walked n this world. At delivery my father had to ay off the midwife and the nurses to keep quiet about my special gift and what sort of person I am. My great grandmother, Patricia, had left many notes and text books for the next witch in the family. It was full of different theories on how to control your powers and how not to reveal yourself as a witch.

The secret behind my mark would have to remain untold as no one except for saving a mortal must a witch reveal her identity, but saving another human has its consequences as your life must be sacrificed unless the human loves you. This situation had happened before with my great grandmother, she healed my great-grandfather from his lengthy battle with cancer but sadly both of their lives were taken by our sworn enemies, the demons that walked upon this world.

The demons have been a witch's sworn enemy since the tale of the demon King, Valkron; he had fallen in love with the witch Gabriella and unfortunately her heart belonged to the mortal Richard Argon. Although this human never knew of Gabriella's existence the demon king took Richard's life to spite Gabriella in the hopes, she will love him once this man was out of the way. But the witch not wanting to lose her love, sacrificed her own life to save Richard's life but because he did not know her, he did not love her back. She was one of the most beautiful witches known of our kind; Richard had wished that he knew who Gabriella was as they could have had a future together. To show his gratitude for Gabriella on saving his life, he paid for a statue of her to be created and placed it in his sacred garden for all eternity. The witch elders cast a spell upon the statue as they feared it would reveal our kind, and to this day the statue stands inside a gazebo on the grounds of a well known park area. The statue of Gabriella can only be seen through the eyes of a witch, any human can not see it. When a demon walks upon the Earth, they disguise themselves as humans so it is often difficult for a witch to detect one but they have a certain scent that only a witch can pick up, this scent is of lust and death.

My parents still wanted me to live a normal life like any other child such as going to school and passing college, I am sure you can imagine what it was like for me during my school days. The other kids took one look at the mark on my right arm and instantly made fun of me, it was worse doing P.E wearing a t-shirt as this would reveal my whole mark. The comments and the laughs did hurt, but I knew one day all these living mortals would need my help. It was just wondering when this situation would happen. I had no friends through school except for Cleo, she seemed to take a liking to me knowing I was different to other kids and often wondered if there was a reason I was born with an enormous mark. Through my years of school I had never socialised with boys apart from the ones who bullied me, I had taken a liking towards a boy called Luke who was in the year above me. He was tall with spikey brown hair and emerald green eyes, his build was very athletic but he did play for the school football team and outside of school hours he was part of a swimming squad at the local leisure centre. From time to time I would go swimming with Cleo on a Friday evening at the swim disco within the leisure centre and I would often see Luke practising his lengths down the far side of the pool away from everyone else but I could never work up the courage to go over and talk to him. I always would hide my right arm under the water for as long as possible to have fewer people staring at my birth mark.

I often wished I had spoken to Luke and got to know him during school, but I thought he would just see me as an outcast like everyone else did. From time to time I thought he was looking at me and smiling but I put it down to him smirking at the fact I had an enormous mark on my right arm. My feelings developed very strongly towards him into falling in love with him, my heart felt like someone had poked it with a pin when Luke had finished school and went onto college. I thought I would never see him again and the day he walked out of the school gates forever I went home that night and cried myself into my pillow, my tears sparkled onto my pillow like spectacles of glitter. Life was strenuous being a witch.

Eventually I was glad to have finished school and looked forward to starting Franklin College this September, I was going to be starting my A-Levels in subjects I wanted to study such as Drama, Dance, English Literature and Media Studies. A fresh start would mean to escape all the torment I had faced and hopefully try to forget all about Luke. My first day of college was just blissful, the atmosphere felt so open and friendly, straight away other people spoke to me normally like I was just like one of them and not an outcast.

After college I would go for a walk to the park and visit the statue of Gabriella, I had called to her the previous night in the hopes she would watch over me starting at college and I wanted to go thank her in my own way. Whilst I was walking out of the primary entrance of the college through the automatic doors I passed Luke without realising it was him. He stopped in my path smiling at me, all the feelings that I had for him went flowing my veins and a warm fuzzy feeling spiralled round in my stomach, of all the places I thought I may bump into him in the future, I would not have expected him to be at the same college as me.

"Hello Precious."

He spoke to me smoothly with a slight charm in the tone of his voice, I could not believe he actually knew who I was.

"Hello Luke, it is nice to see you again. I did not know you went to Franklin College."

He just smiled towards me and for the first time I noticed his dimples on the right side of his cheek, I felt even more drawn towards him and it was like the world around us was empty, that we were the only two people who existed at this moment in time. Everyone else around was just oblivious to us.

"Yes, I have just started my second year doing a course on sports studies."

I kind of knew he would be taking a course that involves sport studies but I thought he may have teamed up with a swimming coach and trained up to hopefully swim as team GB in the Olympics, he had so much potential behind but I did not understand what was holding him back.

"Anyway I have to go but it was nice to see you again Precious."

He smiled towards me again then walked into the college, I just stood for a moment thinking about my feelings of Luke. I wish I could tell him how much I am in love with him but perhaps it would be for the best I kept quiet, if he found out I was a witch then things would only be more complicated and if a demon was nearby, then both mine and Luke's lives could be at risk. I could not let the story of Gabriella be rekindled with my own personal love sick situation, I was not ready to die yet and it would not be fair on Luke to face a near death experience. All these thoughts going through my head gave me a headache, I needed to get to the park for a breather and call to Gabriella.

I set upon my stroll towards the park. The weather was a warm and hazy Indian summer day with a slight breeze in the air. I listened to the birds singing their melodies and the trees whistling their leaves within the wind, I loved hearing Mother Nature on a pleasant day and blessed her kindness with a simple charm I cast from my right arm and to grace her for this glorious day. My middle finger nail slightly glowed as I held my right arm towards the sky and in the distance a rainbow appeared from my cast charm, I looked around just to check nobody saw me but the streets were empty and calm. I felt the wind moving through my long golden hair as though it was being stroked. It was calming and assuring that at this moment in time I was safe.

As I walked onto the park grounds a gust of wind, collected a few fallen leaves and trans-spiralled them gracefully around me, I could see the fountain in the distance sprinkling calmly away and butterflies fluttering by. It was all so calm and tranquil. I walked gracefully along the pavement, I saw families in the distance enjoying the glorious sunshine by playing various games of football and rounders' and I felt a little envious as I never played pleasurable activities with my family. I had no siblings to compete friendly games with and most of my spare time was used to study my gift, it was only the occasional Friday evening when I met up with Cleo but this was still an effort for my parents to even let me leave the house. I knew once I left school that they would calm down a bit more, take a small step back and let me get along on my own two feet. The stroll to the park was such a gift for me that I didn't take the moment for granted.

I wish I had been more alert as I had not realised I was being followed, to make matters worse it was by two male demons disguised as humans. I strolled towards my favourite bench that looked directly at the statue and gazebo. I sat down on the bench to prepare my thoughts to call out for Gabriella but something caught the corner of my eye, Luke was nearby leaning against the tree as though he was in deep thought about something on his mind. He had not seen another human walking towards him with a sword, the blade glistened red like fire and instantly I knew it was a demon heading towards him. My witch instincts took over and took control of my body, my eyes and my birth mark lit up to the sacred golden glow, it now destroyed my tranquil and calm moment. I could not let Luke die, somehow these demons knew of my love towards him and now he was in danger, I screeched out Luke's name in the hopes it would waken him from his deep thought moment. He did not hear me, panic stricken I cast out an earth shake spell to get Luke's attention. The ground beneath him started to shake and rumble. I saw Luke awake upon his deep thinking and look towards me.

"Luke, look out…….. Run!" I yelled out to his direction.

I saw Luke turn around and face towards the raging demon but it was too late, the monster stabbed him through the chest and walked on wiping the blood away from his sword onto his human outfit that the demon was wearing. Luke pained stricken held his chest tightly and collapsed to the ground. My heart began to beat faster and a sharp pain had torn through my heart, he was dying immediately. I looked towards the demon walking away from the scene, the next thing I didn't realise I was doing I was casting the earth shaking spell again but towards the demon this time, the spell was even stronger than before as the pathway developed into a tidal wave and chased the demon. The spell caught hold of the demon and flipped the creature to fall and crash onto the concrete. The demon didn't move so this was my moment to save Luke. I ran towards him as fast as my legs could carry me and allow me to move. Blood had spilled onto the freshly cut green grass and Luke was coughing for air.

"Luke I am so sorry that I have put you through this, please forgive me."
He tried to talk to me but he was in too much pain and blood had filled his lung. It was not clear what he was saying. I held his hands that were still tightly on his wound, I felt the tears fill my eyes and begin to fall down my puffy red cheeks.

"I need you to lay still and trust me. I am going to save your life because I love you."

I kissed his forehead. He was still trying to grasp hold of his life. I removed his hands away from his wound and placed my right hand over it. The ground beneath us felt like it was spinning as a whirl of my healing spell cast a golden and sparkling light around us. I lifted my head up towards the sky and called for Gabriella to grace me with my passing and to protect Luke through the transformation, I knew I was going to die. Luke's wound healed, but the spell had knocked him out. The sky had changed from clear blue to a sudden grey overcast. The park had suddenly been deserted from the families that were playing nearby, I wasn't sure if this was still Earth I was on or the crossing over to the after world and whatever it was I had unfinished business.

The two demons appeared before me, their skin red with fury and their horns as black as night, both of their glances angered me so with all my might and my last breath I moved up onto my feet and stared back at them.

"King Valkon has chosen you." One of them sneered at me.

"Over my dead body." I screeched back at them.

With my deathly minutes drawing closer before my life was over I held my right glowing arm towards the sky, a lightning bolt appeared and struck into my hand. I caught the bolt and zapped it towards the demons. Within a flash the demons evaporated into atoms of dust. I took a deep breath and felt my drained body fall to the ground. My time on this world was over.

My heavy over slept eyes woke up in my bedroom, everything was still in its place except Luke was sat by the desk looking at me. I must have been dreaming, so I rubbed my eyes but again he was still sat there smiling at me.

"Where am I? I am supposed to be dead."

Luke stood up and moved gently towards my bedside. His smile had changed to a more serious look.

"No you are not dead but you have been in a deep sleep for a week, your parents have told me everything about you and all about the sacrifice you did to save my life. I am in love with you to Precious, I always have since the moment I saw you at school."

All this time that I had been worrying what he thought about me was all wrong, he had always felt the same way towards me. He leaned over and kissed me gently on the lips, I felt butterflies fluttering through my stomach and my heart skipped a beat, but I now knew both our lives had changed forever. I remember the words the demon had told me before my spell banished him. I was King Valkon's next chosen mate and he will not stop at nothing until he has me. I gripped Luke at the thought of knowing what my destiny ahead will be.

Spaceman Came Travelling.

This piece is included in Christmas Gifts, first published November 2019. The inspiration for this short story was inspired from Chris De Burgh's song, A Spaceman Came Travelling.

It is always scary being on your own, seeing the days go by one by one, well it is for me, anyway. I can't believe it has been nearly six months since my heart got broken by someone I believed who loved me but instead chose my best friend over me. So I vowed for the time being I wouldn't love anyone on this planet in fear of it happening again. I guess you can still say I am only young and this fool was my first love, being only nineteen I still have a lot to live for. Luckily, I managed to find a small studio and get by working every single hour under the sun. But living this way by being alone did not last much longer for me, I can remember the day when a bright light shone through my window.

It was coming up to Christmas and my full-time office job was forcing me to take annual leave so I had no choice but to take it as my department was shut over the festive period. I had decorated my studio with some tinsel, lights and a small Christmas tree with a star on top of it, in the hopes to make me feel a bit better about myself, I made a wish for the pain I was feeling to go away. Who knew that wishing on a star could come true.

I woke up pulling back my turquoise butterfly patterned curtains to a snowy Christmas Eve morning, late morning to be precise but I think it was more lunch time as the night before I had watched a few chick flicks and downed a bottle of pink gin. I lifted my head up from off my pillow to the worse hangover I had ever encountered. Stumbling to the little kitchen area, I downed a glass of water trying to come to my senses.

Later on that evening my hangover had eased off, so I managed to get out of my slump to go outside. The snow had slowed down and come to a stop by the time I got outside; I gazed up to the starry night sky and seeing how the stars were trying to break through the snow clouds. In the distance I heard a choir singing from a nearby Church 'Silent Night, Holy Night.' As I was listening to the lyrics and gazing upwards, a light flew across between the snowy clouds. 'Perhaps that was a shooting star.' I thought to myself, but it seemed to near, so close. It was most likely my heavy hungover head playing tricks on me. I decided to head back home and call it an early one in bed.

That night I was woken up by a bright light shining through my window, I did not realise what time it was, it could not have possibly be the morning already. I ran over to the nearest window, but the light was too bright for me.Then suddenly I was standing on the roof of the building I lived in, I didn't even know how I had gotten up there. I looked around to see a figure standing before me, he was the most beautiful guy I had ever seen. I did not understand where he appeared from, but I could not help myself but stare at him. How embarrassing for me though as I was wearing my unicorn pyjamas, but he didn't seem to mind what I was wearing as he just looked into my eyes. His eyes were hazel coloured, and his skin sparkled upon the light that was shining above us. It was like a flying saucer object just hovering over us.

He pulled me closer to him, his hair was chocolate brown, slightly spikey. For a moment there was no words that I could bring myself to say or ask him. There was something about him that was just out of this world. "Hello." His voice sounded as graceful as an angel. Then reality hit me as I felt scared and started to shake. "Please don't be afraid of me, do not fear." It was like he was trying to make me calm down. "Who are you?" I finally managed to say something to him. "I am just like you, I have travelled from afar searching for you." This was sounding crazy, but I liked it, I didn't care if it was just a dream or my hangover still taking over me but in this very moment my heartache had just vanished.

"You are just beautiful." Was all I could say back to him. He placed his lips so tenderly onto mine and I didn't want this moment to end. My head then got the better of me as it felt so heavy, I felt his hands catch my fall but still everything went black.

I woke up on Christmas day, another late morning, only this time I was feeling so alive and so fresh. It was like I had become a whole new person after my visit from a spaceman the night before. I had decided to get up and open up presents from my parents that I had put under my little Christmas tree.

There was one that I had not seen before, wrapped in sparkly silver paper and tied with a silver bow. The label read:

I will return again
Merry Christmas
Love from your Spaceman.

Feel the Thunder.

1.

It was just like any normal typical English weather day during the month of April; the rain was pouring fast and drumming loudly onto the rooftops. Gloomy clouds formed through the sky over the town as though it was appearing to cover the area, so no light could break through. The sound of the flood sirens can be heard for miles upon miles, warning if a light possibility that a tidal wave may erupt through the town causing the area to flood. A busy old looking Victorian warehouse located five miles away from the town in the middle of nowhere stood alone; inside the warehouse it had been converted into a polythene factory. This is one of many businesses the town's welfare depended on. The only other building next to the warehouse was a newly built office block.

Kimberly sat at her desk looking out of the office window, her blonde hair pinned up tightly to form a bun. Her chipped red nails tapping viciously onto the varnished, stained wooden desk, her eyes gazing into nothing. "Kimberly, wake up." A woman's voice was heard, Kimberly's gaze is interrupted, and she looks round the office to the direction where the voice appeared from. The other woman is a little older than Kimberly, her name is Jane.

"Sorry Jane." Kimberly replies half asleep from a wonderful daydream that consisted of her meeting the love of her life. Kimberly never seems to have much luck with men; she has got the looks, the figure, the personality and the fashion sense. The poor girl just can never date a man that she can click with and hopefully one day settle down with. "perhaps I should go out and get some air."

Slowly, like a snail lifting herself up off the desk chair, Kimberly smiles at Jane and leaves the office gracefully. She strolls towards the door that leads her to the stairs upon the back entrance of the factory. Clink clonk is the sound her heeled shoes creates heading down the stairs and the loud machinery is heard upon the entrance of the factory. The raindrops hitting the roof mixes along with the sound of the machines, this is about as loud as a heavy metal band at a gig and the smell of burning plastic filled the air.

Suddenly a tremendous flash of light hit the factory followed by a loud bang, the roof caved in and the ground shook as though the building had been struck by a thunder storm. Panicked workmen sprinted out of the factory to escape from the colliding roof. Kimberly looked around in anixously; her feet felt as though she was stuck to the floor like glue and she began to hyperventilate in fear that she was going to not live past this event. Colossal pieces of roof tiles and glass fell to the fall, surrounding her ability to escape.

"Help!!!" Kimberly screams out at the top of her lungs, but there is no one around to save her. Kimberly's head felt heavy, her eyes closed, and she fell to the ground. Just before Kimberly hits the ground, someone out of nowhere approaches her and grasps hold of her to prevent her from falling on the factory floor. Through semi-consciousness eyes, Kimberly faces the mysterious person and she can just about make out his eyes. They are the colour blue, south sea blue and very magical; it is as though Kimberly felt like she was being drawn into his embrace. "Stay with me." Were the words she just about could make out, his voice sounded deep but soft and then suddenly everything went black, Kimberly lost her vision and she could no longer see the mystery man's fascinating blue eyes.

Kimberly woke up early the next morning in hospital with her vision returned but there was no memory of the event from the previous day, there was an uncomfortable feeling from her right arm where a tube appeared to have been injected into it which was connected to a liquid bag. The bed she was laying on felt stiff and very firm, as if it was cardboard the mattress was produced from. The pillows were not puffy feathered ones like she had at home, it was like her head was resting on a bag of straw that were wrapped in white nylon cloth.

Kimberly looked around the compact room; she had been placed in a private sector. The light in the room was dazzling, it was too bright that Kimberly had to squint her recently returned vision. The smell in the air was clean but slightly chemical, more like the smell of disinfectant along with the slight linger of burnt toast. This was most likely came from the kitchen. Kimberly had a thought to herself, the light being so bright and the smell of something burning. Holy crap, what had happened at the factory?

The thought of remembering the factory collapsing round her brought a shiver down her spine, "I could have died in there." She spoke out loud to herself in a panic. Kimberly glances round the room again, she notices the curtains are faded blue and hung one side on a curtain tail that goes round the position of where the hospital bed is placed. The thought of blue eyes and the mystery man triggers back into her mind, she sighs to calm herself down, just remembering him again makes her feel at ease. Who was he? She thought again to herself. From what she recalls there was no one around, then suddenly as things went dark and feeling faint, this person appeared from nowhere.

Her thought process is interrupted by the door to her room opening; a nurse quietly walks into the room to check on Kimberly, expecting her to still be asleep. The nurse smiles at her. "Good to see your now awake Miss Lowe. The doctor will come and see you shortly; he just wants to carry out a couple of tests before a decision is made to discharge you."

"How did I get here?" Asked Kimberly trying to sound confused and puzzled. "Everyone had left me inside the factory, I was trapped." The nurse just kindly smiled at her, "Oh no they found you unconscious outside the factory."

"I must have hit my head when I fainted as I can't really remember how I got out of there." Even though Kimberly knew full well how she managed to have escaped from the factory, her mission now was to find this mystery man and discover his identity.

2.

At the site where the factory previously was, detectives and forensics were hard at work investigating what had happened and what caused the lightning and thunder to target the factory. Tremendous masses of rubble, dust and metal surrounded the site; as if nothing could have survived the collapsed factory. The smell of burnt wood lingered the area still even though there was no fire active at this moment in time, unaware to the detectives was someone in the shadows watching their every move.

"I have found a stiletto shoe." Shouts one of the detectives. He was standing in the position where Kimberly had her episode with the mysterious man. "I think it is the shoe from the survivor Miss Lowe, who is currently in hospital. But how did she escape before the building collapsed over her? The position where this shoe is to where she was found outside shows she would not have made it in time. I think we need to send an officer to obtain a statement from her."

"I think she has been discharged already, I shall radio the station now to find her whereabouts and for all patrolling officers to keep a look out."

The figure in the shadows overhears the conversation between the detectives to search for Kimberly; he moves away rapidly from the factory site and sprints to the hills heading towards the local town. The person in the shadow's is Kimberly's mystery man.

Kimberly waited patiently outside the hospital for her taxi to arrive; she needed the fresh air to try help focus her mind on the recent events. But the memory of the mystery man and his south sea-blue eyes would not leave her alone. Just thinking of him gave a warm fuzzy feeling inside making her feel safe. The sound of an ambulance siren interrupted her thought process, the ambulance raced past Kimberly and headed onto the main road. The taxi appears to be taking too long. She looks at her pandora watch with a purple strap on it, the strap is covered in dust and the face of the watch has a crack on it. 'Damn, I love this watch and now it is ruined.' Kimberly thought to herself, she felt quite disheartened that her favourite watch had been wrecked. In her irritated mood, Kimberly is bored of waiting for the taxi, so she decides a gracious walk home will calm her down.

The weather was warm, the sun glowed through the sky and there appeared to not be a black cloud in site compared to how the weather was the day before and the monstrous thunderstorm that erupted the town and caused the factory to collapse. The smell of fresh cut grass filled the air. The local residents were taking advantage of the lovely weather to mow their lawns and small groups of families set up picnics in the local park.

The park was a beautiful and very scenic area, there were trees planted throughout the park and a stream flowed through the centre. The sound of trickling water was heard throughout the park, there was a water feature right in the centre of the stream that appeared to have a statue of an ancient God holding a hammer, there was a plaque by the stream that read 'Feel The Thunder.' On another plaque located further along the park read the words 'Thor: God Of Thunder and Lightning.'

As the park is round the corner from the hospital and leads to a pathway towards Kimberly's apartment, she decided to take a pleasant stroll through the beautiful and scenic area. Kimberly always loved walking through the park come rain or shine; it was as though this was her safe haven to be whenever she had an awful day at work to mending a broken heart from past disappointing relationships. This time round Kimberly stopped and admired the statue of the ancient god. She had all the time in the world at this moment. She gazed upon the stone feature of Thor and smiled with a slight blush in her cheeks. "If only." She spoke out loud to herself.

Suddenly two patrolling police officers approached Kimberly; she was still in a daze with the statue that she hadn't noticed the officers standing side by side of her. "Excuse me Miss?" said the female officer in a stern voice, "we need you to come with us." Still Kimberly was in a world of her own, she hadn't noticed the police were talking to her. Whilst in her day dream world she heard the mystery man's voice 'Kimberly, you are in danger. Wake up, please.' It was as though he spoke to her standing by her side, his voice still sounded so deep but soft however this time there was a tone of anxiety with his words. As though she actually was in danger, instead of a warm fuzzy feeling inside, she felt an icy chill shiver down her spine. She woke up back at the park facing the statue. Both of the police officers were still standing side by side.

"Sorry officers, I was in a world of my own." She spoke with a tone sounding ditzy, but inside it worried her. 'Perhaps he can see me now?' Kimberly questioned to herself. This time the police officers did not respond, looking straight at the police woman there was something strange about her eyes. They were not human, just black, Cosmic black, no pupils, iris or sclera could be seen like on a human eye. "What or who are you?" asked a shaken and terrified Kimberly.

"You need to come with us." Hissed the other officer, his voiced sounded not human but as though he was a snake trapped in a human's body. The creatures both reached out to grab Kimberly; their grasp felt so tight as though they were trying to cut off the blood circulation to her arms and their palms felt ice cold. She tried to struggle but their grasp got even tighter, Kimberly surrendered and just flopped herself in their clutches.

3.

From out of nowhere the ground shook and a sonic boom sound erupted through the air. The sky suddenly changed from glorious sunshine with a clear sky to dull and thick tenorite grey clouds and no rays of the sun breaking through. "Let her go." A voice appeared from nowhere, Kimberly looks around but no one else can be seen. The two officers get agitated but still remain holding the poor girl. A figure approaches towards them holding a hammer; he has a bright glow surrounding him. Kimberly notices him; from a distance, she could make out the south sea-blue eyes. A warm fuzzy feeling fills her inside again. It was her heroic mystery man that only saved her life yesterday and is now coming to her aid again. The closer he got the more she could make him out, he was everything she imagined him to be. Short blonde clean cut hair, broad muscular frame, and his face was clean shaven. He wore Viking style armour. Kimberly noticed the statue out of the corner of her eye and saw how familiar it looked to her mystery man. 'It can't be?' She thought to herself, but the more she looked the more true it appeared to her.

"It's Thor." Shouted the female officer, "Get him." The other officer charged towards the almighty god, Thor stopped in his tracks and stood firm, hammer at the grip of his hand. The hammer lit up; it shone a diamond white glow, as the hammer lit up it retracted a lightning bolt and struck it straight into the charging creature. The officer flew back and landed right through a nearby tree, the body remained lifeless however a black but see through cloud spirit flew out and charged towards Thor again. However Thor remained still in his stance and was not afraid to challenge this thing again, he held his posture until the right moment came to attack it. The lightning bolt zapped back towards Thor, catching the spirit on its path, the spirit vaporised into thousands of dust particles.

The other police officer closely observed what happened to her companion; she released Kimberly from her clutches and sprinted away in the opposite direction. Thor saw her trying to get make a run for it. He sprinted and flew past Kimberly and caught up with the evil creature in a blink of an eye. He grasped hold of the police officer and looked at her straight in the face; she squeals out an ear deafening sound. Thor grabs hold of her throat to silence the squealing sound.

"No use calling for help, I will only destroy each and every one of you who thinks of taking Kimberly away. Now go back to where you came from and never bother her again." The body becomes lifeless in Thor's hand; another cloud, spirit flew out of the body and approached Kimberly. However Thor caught hold of it and spun it round, he then threw it up to the cloud ridden sky where it flew off out of sight to escape.

The clouds then suddenly released the sun's rays and gold strands appeared in the sky. It was as though Thor had controlled the weather. Even the butterflies and other wildfire came to grace us with their presence. Kimberly starred for a moment at him feeling shocked but also inside feeling happy. He had saved her life again. The thunder god strolled quickly towards her and for a moment the pair of them look into each other's eyes.

"It's you from yesterday, you saved my life." She spoke to him; Thor smiled and held her in his powerful embrace. "What's been happening?"

"For the past couple of months I have been watching you from afar, those creatures were disguising themselves as police officers. They are known as the Raids and are evil spirits from the Dark Lands."

"Where are the Dark Lands?" asked a confused Kimberly.

"The Dark Lands is home to the enemies of myself and my father Odin, we have a truce with them at the moment that no one from Asgard or the Dark Lands is to bring war again.

But it seems like some of the Raids is now causing this to happen again."

"What do they want from me though?"

"To cause a war, they need a human sacrifice and unfortunately their oracle has predicted your soul to be the best sacrifice to cause a war, bring on an apocalypse to this world and turn it into the new Dark Lands. Yesterday they planned to kidnap you at the factory so I came to stop them, but on my way down to Earth those two Raids attacked me which caused me to fall in the factory and accidently destroy it."

"Well at least you have got me some time off work." Giggles Kimberly to Thor and trying to bring some light heart on the situation, they both glance at each other for a moment. His lips then softly touch hers, his mouth felt warm and tender, he brushes his hands through her blonde and stringy hair. She held on to him tightly, Kimberly knew he would not be able to stay with her and that he would have to go back to Asgard.

"I have to go back for a little while, I need to speak with my father and update him on this situation. But I promise I will be back in no time, please keep yourself safe but I will be watching over you."

Tears start to fill her eyes but she knew this is the only way for them to be together. He holds her for a moment and kisses her again. The sun began to fall to let the moon take over the sky. As dusk appeared Thor released Kimberly from his embrace.

"I promise I will come back for you." He spoke deeply but softly. He then trudged down the path, Kimberly watched him walk away until he was no longer in sight. The tears that filled her eyes now began to fall down her warm rosy cheeks. She looked up at the sky and noticed a shooting red light head to the sky. It was Thor going back to Asgard.

"Please come back soon." She spoke out loud. "I will wait for you."

The Eve of Christmas

This short story is also included in Christmas Gifts, first published November 2019.

It hardly ever snowed on Christmas Eve in England, especially on the coastal town of Cleethorpes, however mother nature decided to grant us all an early gift for a white Christmas. As there was no school because of the winter break I had the chance to go and explore the area all covered in white. There had been a good six inches of snow that'd fallen from the early hours of the morning. My parents had left yesterday to go visit my grandparents, but I chose to stay at home to look after our pet dog, Hunnie. She was a Staffordshire bull terrier, just vaguely a puppy with light golden brown fur with a white fur chest. Before my parents left, my mother gave me a couple of dos and don'ts round the house, although I was seventeen she still treated me like a child.

"Also Eve. Last of all, no parties." She told me before they were on their way.

Today I was taking Hunnie on my brief adventure out into the snow. This was the first time she had ever stepped foot on the white ice cold substance. Wrapping up warm in my UGG boots and thick woollen coat with a butterfly styled woollen hat with matching scarf. I had put on a little doggy coat for Hunnie too. We made our way towards the seafront. The snow had stopped falling by the time we headed outside, along Cambridge street up to the promenade area. There were hardly any moving cars on the road, nature had taken its cause to blanket the roads over. Anyone who'd tried to drive in this weather, they were stuck on the intact snow along the edges of the road. As I walked by the street, I noticed the welcoming light of the Globe Coffee shop, I thought to myself that I would head there after our brief walk.

As we reached the barrier to the sea wall, the clouds opened and let the thick snowdrops fall again only this time they were twice as thick. The wind blew strongly along with the fallen snow, I tried to look down at Hunnie who was struggling to walk through the elements. I picked her up and hurried us quickly as I could towards the Globe. The owner had spotted us approaching through the big open window and kindly opened the front door for me before I got there.

"Are you both alright?" the owner kindly asked me.

I nodded at him through shivering teeth and sitting down at a large vintage table. The owner was called Matthew, he was such a kind and welcoming gentleman. Through his spectacles, he always had friendly, and caring eyes for each customer. He placed a menu down in front of me.

"You are my first customer today, take your time, get warm and I will be back over soon to collect your order."

I gazed through each word on the menu deciding what to have, I felt the heating round the room soothe my cold muscles, as I gradually got warm I removed my coat, gloves, and hat. Hunnie was good as gold and just laid on the floor rolled up into a ball, then eventually into a snore as she drifted off to sleep. The heat was then interrupted as the front door flew open and entered what I thought was a snowman. Whoever it was brushed the snow off himself to reveal one of the cutest guys I went to school with. It was Adam, I had a crush on him since we started school together those few years ago. The weather was really coming down thick and fast. Adam acknowledged me and sat down at the far side of my table.

"If it carries on like this, you might be stuck in here for the rest of the day," I heard Matthew call to us from behind the counter.

I just giggled at his comment, but I sort of hoped that would not happen as I wanted to be back home in my nice warm house. I did not live too far away, but the weather looked dreadful and not safe to be heading back home. I gazed out of the window and in such a brief space of time the snow blizzard had completely covered the majority of the glass frame.

"Don't worry I have a spare room upstairs you can all stay in." he kindly offered to us.

"Thank you." I smiled gratefully to him.

Adam had now warmed up, so he gradually removed his coat, gloves and beanie hat and looked down at the menu.

"I'm going to have the New York pancake stack with a luxury hot chocolate." I mentioned to him. His eyes then moved up to look at me, and he smiled.

"That sounds good, I am going to have the same."

Matthew had heard us so he went away into the kitchen area to prepare our orders, during this time I had a little catch up with Adam.Iit had been over a week since I last saw him at school and during our final period together we had a brief moment in English. During the class, we were discussing what Christmas and the festive season meant to us, Adam was sat next to me and I felt him gently touch my left hand. I looked round at him and he whispered softly into my ear, 'Have a wonderful Christmas, Eve. I will miss you.' His gentle and caring words touched me, these had stayed with me the past week playing that moment over and over in my head. Now the spirit of Christmas had granted me an early wish, which was to see him again.

"I am so glad you are here." I said to him.

"Me too." He took my right hand into his. "I have not stopped thinking about you since we finished school."

This was my eve of Christmas to remember forever.

Her - A Vigilante in the Making.

When the going gets tough, the tough indeed will get going. I may be a woman but I know how to whoop some backside, any villain who approaches me will wish they had not dared to cross my path. Who needs Wonder Woman or Black Widow when you can have..... oh bugger, what could I call myself? Here I was standing in front of my full-length mirror admiring my new found lease of life, recently I had been involved in a vigilante act stopping a pair of bank robbers known as Bob and Frank. Since I had finished in nappies as an infant my parents signed me up to all these different martial arts classes. Karate, Kick Boxing and Taekwondo just to name a few, I had undergone strict regimes from what I eat up to the point of socialising, I barely had a social life apart from when I was in school. Boys.. whoever had time for boys and kissing behind the back of the bike shed. The only bit of eye candy for me was those muscular, toned men during my martial arts classes. One guy I never could keep my eyes off was my sensei, Paul, I loved it when he was topless in the dojo. He was older than me, 24 years old. I had only just finished sixth form. Ok, focus now if I want to get my head into being a vigilante in my local town.

Searching through my wardrobes trying to arrange an outfit that I could easily wear to fight in... erm that is too baggy, no that is too dressy, ah yes this catsuit will do. I gaze and grasp through the leathery material, deciding what to alter. Of course I don't want to copy the black canary wearing an all in one catsuit. I needed to think fast as the breaking news of today was that Bob and Frank had been released on bail so who knew what they could be planning to do tonight. Perhaps I could cut a bit out on the left hip or waist side, maybe even round the thigh area. I would like to keep my arms fully covered though, I don't want anyone to see my purple and turquoise butterfly tattoo. Ah yes I know just the thing, I will cut slits up on both sides of the legs and add zips, I need to add a bit of glamour to my appearance. Eye mask at the ready and bright red lip stick, I must remember to not kiss my beaten up villains, can't leave any DNA lying about now. No one must know who I am. Time to go find those divvy pair of dumb ass robbers. One problem, does my bum look big in this?

It did not take me long to track them down, all I did was head to the nearest bank and one they had not yet destroyed. Hiding behind a nearby parked up van, I waited for my right moment to sneak up on them.

"Yo Bob, get ya arse in gear and find a way to get inside."

That was Frank's voice. How stupid could he get yelling that out. It may be past midnight but do they not realise someone could be watching them. I climbed gracefully under the van to try watch what these pair of nit wits were doing. Bob scurried to the back of a nearby parked up car and into the boot, pulled out a battering ram. He then vanished round the back of the building and within five minutes he was opening the front door to let in Frank. This was now my cue to do something, it was so easy last time trying to fight these two so I am sure it will be a walk in the park again. I back flipped gracefully across the road, took a quick glance round to check the coast was still clear and followed Frank close behind entering the building.

This time they were more alert and must have expected company. Perhaps these two were not as dumb as they seem to be.

"Shit Frank, I think it is her again."

"Lets get her." Yelled Frank.

The two of them charged towards me at the same time, I had to make a quick decision on my move, it was now or never. Both guys were now standing side by side of me about to throw punches, I slipped my right leg forward and left leg behind. Split dodge, the advantage of wearing a skin tight cat suit and being very flexible. Bob and Frank ended up punching each other. If I could have stopped and laughed at them I would have but there was no time for that. Swirling my left leg round I tripped up Frank, he landed on the ground in a pile creating a loud thud. I landed my feet flat on the ground and made eye contact with Bob, rubbing his chin from where Frank's punch knocked him, he charged towards me again. I blocked his fist and instant reaction I gave him an upper cut to the ribs with some force. It hurt my knuckles like hell, but I saw how much more pain he was in.

"Ouch, I broke a nail." Whoops, I shouldn't have spoken, now they know what my voice sounds like.

"What's going on here?" a male voice I did not recognise.

I looked round to see a security guard in the distance and the sound of sirens fast approaching, I could not let the police catch me in the act.

Red.

Starting college was something I had been dreading all summer, no more acting like a child for me. I would meet many strangers and hoped they would turn into friends of mine where we could support and guide each other through our studies. I was starting a diploma in dance; I had always wanted to be a dancer all the way through school and I had high hopes that I would eventually be cast onto a West End show. The day was the second of September, but my college years would be a time in my life that I would never forget. It was a time where strange encounters happened with me, knowing that magic existed and fairy tales really do truly happen. Although the day was warm and hazy like an Indian summer's day with butterflies still fluttering around in the gentle breeze, I still chose to wear my red coat that my grandmother gifted for me for my birthday. I could hear the words of passers-by call me 'Red Riding Hood.' I had just moved to the area to live with my grandparents as my grandmother hadn't been too well, or so I thought.

Walking along the newly painted corridor, still smelling the fresh coating in the air, I hadn't noticed him following me. The fumes had got to me a bit too much and took over my senses which made me not realise I was being stalked at this moment in time. I approached the locker area trying to remember the pass code I was sent via email, as my hands were full of books and carrying an enormous shoulder bag I did not want to start rummaging to dig out my phone. Feeling unevenly balanced from everything I was carrying and the fumes of whatever the maintenance staff had used to coat the walls, I started to become very heavy headed and losing my balance. I closed my eyes to prepare myself to hit the ground where out of nowhere he appeared and caught hold of me. He was a couple of years older than me, but one of the first things I noticed was on his right shoulder was a tattoo of a white wolf howling up at the moon. I gazed at the colours of his tattoo and I could have sworn the image slightly moved but I had put it down to feeling fuzzy headed.

I was drawn to this mysterious guy from this very moment, he had hazel cynical eyes and chocolate spiked hair that tempted me to touch it, as he looked down at me and smiled, a dimple appeared on his right cheek. He was just so cute, gorgeous in fact. I never felt like this before about any guy, not through school as I just saw them as total losers. It was like something over the summer, and being in a new town had changed me.

Barge and the fly

I gaze out the window of an old barge boat now converted as a bar upon a calm river, sipping from a water-stained glass that is filled to the brim with sweet fizzy cola. I had only just turned eighteen, but the day was still young. The air is calm and tranquil with a faint sound of rock music just about interfering with my quiet moment I am having. Upon my gaze a young, handsome guy crosses my eyeline in the distance as he is walking over to his silver Mini Cooper. My eyes follow the direction where he is heading and as he reaches his vehicle, his eyes meet mine for a brief moment. I smile, he nods and then enters his vehicle. He drives slowly away until I can no longer have a visual of the silver car. Oh, what a lovely brief encounter that was. My moment is then interrupted by a buzzing sound, a pesky fly right by my ear and no doubt the damn thing is after my cola. I waft it gently away and with luck the fly moves towards the open window and buzzes off. Thank goodness the cola is still all mine. I turn around gracefully to the table where my drink is and as coincidence shows to me, a poster on the wall catches my eye stating 'Time Flies.' I giggle to myself in the funny moment reading the poster when suddenly the irritating buzzing sound is back. I move my head in the direction to come face to face with that pesky fly again.

I try flicking the fly away but its attempt to take my sweet drink from me is its key priority, it dodges my hand and quickly flies over to my glass. Why couldn't it just have been a butterfly instead as for sure it would not be irritating me to get to my drink? It lands on the rim and begins circling round the glass, I quickly move my thumb and finger to try grab the damn thing but the little sod is too quick for me and enters the inside of the glass. Heading to my sweet cola I try grabbing the fly again and to my advantage luck was on my side as I finally have hold of it. Haha I win little fly as that cola is mine. Suddenly the glass slips over from underneath me and falls right into my lap. No more sweet cola for me. Bye bye drink and hello to sticky jeans. Ok Mr Fly you may have won this battle, but the war is far from over.

My First.

An excellent idea just came to mind as though I had just lit a light bulb, yes the idea was going to be amazing. I jumped onto my bicycle and hit the road, I just had to share my opinion with someone. I biked up to the nearest bus shelter and right on cue there he was, Tom, the one I would share my amazing idea with. The idea that had just come to mind as easy as lighting up a light bulb that made me jump onto my bicycle to the nearest bus shelter to see Tom.

"Tom, I have the best idea to tell you." I said, all giddy.

"Go on, be quick as my college bus will be here any minute." He said with a smile.

"Tom, I love you. I want you to be my first." I blurted it out before realising there was a crowd at the bus shelter. Tom went bright red as a tomato. Nerves hit me, I felt a strange sensation in my stomach as though I had butterflies in there fluttering around.

"I will speak to you later about our.... Erm... situation." The bus then pulled up, and he made a quick getaway to jump on the bus.

Isolation

Day One

My first day being stuck inside these four brick walls. Recently our country was diseased by a plague virus concocted by the DNA of vermin. It is lead to believe that this virus is manmade, created in a laboratory somewhere in the world and has been given the nickname of ZOVI. Yesterday my college was forced to close for the safety of the students and our tutors. Someone had come to the premises severely infected from ZOVI. A student who did not understand what he was doing approached the primary entrance of the college campus. I was just in his eye site where he tackled me to the ground and took a chunk out of my arm. He was sweating feverishly along with the reddest of blood-shot eyes I had ever seen. My mum was called instantly, she is a scientist so now it was her mission to find a cure. Wrong place, wrong time to be, I guess.

Day Five.

Today they have shipped me from the comfort of my own home to a secure safe house. I am under full surveillance for twenty-four hours. I haven't seen or spoken to my mum since she went into work five days ago. I know she is working hard to try to find a cure for me. Symptoms check, I am starting to feel a burning sensation round my cheeks and my forehead is dripping droplets of sweat. I also found out today that the prime minister has ordered the country to go into full lockdown until further notice. Last time I saw my friends was six days ago, I am missing them so deeply. At seventeen I should be hanging out with them, not locked away like some animal in a cage.

My insides begin to erupt, I can sense I will throw up. I have eaten nothing today so I hope it will just be some bile. As I make it to the nearest toilet, I lean over the porcelain bowl and let out what my stomach needs to. However, the taste in my mouth was more metallic than acidy. A quick glance to my stomach contents revealed a dark red gloopy substance. Blood. Suddenly someone in a biohazard suit rushes in and instantly injects something into my neck. Before I come to terms with what is happening, everything goes black.

Day Ten.

I am still locked away in this safe house and my every move is being watched. Since five days ago I have only had the one bio-suit visitor come in to see me and inject the usual area on my neck. They believe it is slowing down the spread of this virus round my body. I just hope my mum and her team hurry up and find me a cure to reverse whatever is happening to me. My heart is beating faster than normal but they have assured me this is anxiety and not relating to this virus.

I am sick of pot noodles and pasta now, especially mac and cheese, but I do have a continuous supply of toilet roll. I miss being out and about, even cabin fever is kicking in. The surface of my skin burned up again today, splashing cool water over my face I take a glance at myself in the mirror. My skin colour has turned a faint grey along with my left eye looking abnormal, it is bloodshot fully. Then next up my insides turn on me again and I just want to throw up, as before my stomach contents have revealed red, blood.

Day Fifteen.

They have since upped my dosage on this trial injection to try to slow down the ZOVI virus but it is leaving me all drowsy. I am choosing to stay in today as I have woken up with bad period cramps. I am in too much discomfort to eat or move about today.

Day Twenty.

I haven't washed my hair in five days; it is like someone has poured oil all over my head. My hair is all clumpy and every time I stroke my hands through my hair, it is like touching straw. I have to force myself out of bed and crawl to the nearest bathroom. For the majority of today I spent it in the shower.

Day Thirty.

The news I have been waiting patiently for, success a cure has been found but grim news is I have to wait another week for it to finally get to me. Whilst I have been in lockdown the prime minister sadly got infected too. I have missed being able to go outside to breathe in the fresh air, feeling the sun's rays and seeing the butterflies flying around in the meadows. So the first vaccination is to be given to the prime minister, but also I have since been informed of the news that my father is responsible for all of this, he created the virus out of spite on my mother leaving him all those years ago. Once I am cured and out of this holding facility, I aim to find my father and punish him for this.

Acknowledgments

A little bit about myself, I live in the town of Grimsby where I work full time at a car dealership and in my spare time I love to write and read many wonderful books. Over the years, I have attended two evening writing courses at the Grimsby Institute (2013 and 2017). During the summer of July 2018 I started going to a weekly writers group (on Tuesdays) held at the Barge Inn, this group was formed by a writer called Ruth. Unfortunately, Ruth could not continue the writers group into 2019 so myself and a handful of the regular writers formed up our own writing group which is held at The Globe.

First of all thank you so much for reading my anthology of short stories and flash fiction, as I have written a fair few I wanted to include a handful of them into my own book.

I would also like to say thank you to my family, and to my fiancé for all of their support over the years on the many hobbies I have tried to accomplish, I promise them that writing will be the one I will be sticking to.

Thank you to Matthew Head, the owner of the Globe Coffee shop in Cleethorpes, without his support, the Globe Writers group would not have a weekly venue to meet up and write. I would like to thank all the writers from this group but especially Ants Ambridge. Without his help and guidance, my anthology would never have happened.

Last of all I would like to say a big thank you to the bookstagram community on Instagram. I have spoken to many lovely bookstagrammers over the last couple of years.

Gemma has also been featured in the following anthologies.

Monday At Six - first published in October 2017, available on Amazon and Kindle

Fish and Freaks - first published in October 2018, available on Amazon and Kindle

Christmas Gifts - first published in November 2019, available on Amazon and Kindle. The royalties from this anthology are donated to Lincs and Notts Air Ambulance.

Printed in Poland
by Amazon Fulfillment
Poland Sp. z o.o., Wrocław

58238682R00073